TOO
Small
Tola
Makes It **Count**

Books by the same author

Too Small Tola
Too Small Tola and the Three Fine Girls
Too Small Tola Gets Tough

Anna Hibiscus
Hooray for Anna Hibiscus!
Good Luck, Anna Hibiscus!
Have Fun, Anna Hibiscus!
Welcome Home, Anna Hibiscus!
Go Well, Anna Hibiscus!
Love from Anna Hibiscus!
You're Amazing, Anna Hibiscus!

The No. 1 Car Spotter
The No. 1 Car Spotter and the Firebird
The No. 1 Car Spotter and the Car Thieves
The No. 1 Car Spotter Goes to School
The No. 1 Car Spotter and the Broken Road
The No. 1 Car Spotter Fights the Factory

For younger readers
Anna Hibiscus' Song
Splash, Anna Hibiscus!
Double Trouble for Anna Hibiscus!
Baby Goes to Market
B Is for Baby
Baby, Sleepy Baby
Catch That Chicken!
Hugo

Non-fiction
Africa, Amazing Africa: Country by Country

TOO
Small
Tola
Makes It Count

ATINUKE

illustrated by
ONYINYE IWU

WALKER
BOOKS

For Tiger and Noa.

A.

To Sharon and Yvonne. Thank you.

O.I.

The right of Atinuke and Onyinye Iwu to be identified as author and illustrator respectively of this work has been asserted in accordance with the Copyright, Designs and Patents Act 1988

This book has been typeset in Stempel Schneidler

Printed and bound by CPI Group (UK) Ltd, Croydon CR0 4YY

British Library Cataloguing in Publication Data: a catalogue record for this book is available from the British Library

ISBN 978-1-4063-9938-7

www.walker.co.uk

MIX
Paper | Supporting responsible forestry
FSC® C171272

CONTENTS

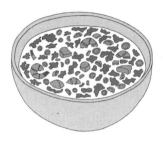

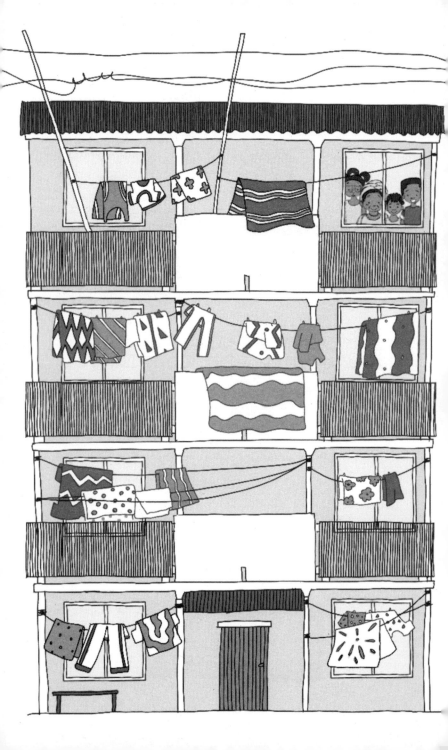

Grandmummy

Tola

Moji

Dapo

Tola Finds a Solution

Tola lives in a run-down block of flats in the megacity of Lagos, in the country of Nigeria.

She lives with her sister, Moji, her brother, Dapo, and Grandmummy. Grandmummy is the boss of them all.

Tola has lived with Moji, Dapo and Grandmummy since the day she was born.

But when the virus came to Lagos and lockdown happened, then everything changed.

Moji went to live at her teacher's house so she could continue her school work. Dapo went to live at the garage so he could continue training to be a mechanic. And Tola went to work as a house girl for a rich family called the Diamonds because she and Grandmummy had no money for food.

Tola not only worked there – she lived there too, because that is what house girls do!

Now Tola does not have to live with the Diamonds any more. She has agreed to work for them on Saturdays but not until they get back from their stay in London.

Now lockdown is over and Moji and Dapo and Tola are home. They and Grandmummy are so so happy!

"Moji!" Grandmummy orders. "Help me grind the beans for

the moi-moi!"

"Dapo!" Grandmummy orders. "Help me collect a newspaper from the hawkers."

"Tola!" Grandmummy orders. "Help me measure how much material I have here." When Grandmummy says "help me" she means "do it for me right now!"

But Moji and Dapo and Tola don't mind. They are too happy to mind anything now that they are home and all together.

Every poor person in Lagos is rejoicing that lockdown is over. Now they can go out into the city and earn money without the police chasing them back. All Tola's neighbours are out in the corridors celebrating.

"It was hard-o! It was hard!" claims Mama Business.

Mama Business has children in the UK. They sent her money so she did not have to leave the flats even once during lockdown.

"But we managed, we managed." Mr Abdul smiles gently.

Mr Abdul had to go to work every day or his family would have starved. He was chased home by the police more times than he can remember.

"Some of us," he says, looking at Tola. "Some of us even triumphed."

"Some of us are liars!" The Ododi boy mocks.

The Ododi boy does not believe that Tola worked for the Diamonds. The Diamonds are the most uber-mega-famous Afrobeat musicians in Nigeria. There is no way Too Small Tola could have worked for them.

Mr Abdul turns away from the Ododi boy.

He always turns away from angry people. But Tola's brother Dapo does not.

"Who are you calling a liar?" He asks angrily.

Grandmummy steps between them.

"Dapo," she orders. "Help me fetch me my fan. I am sweating."

Dapo hesitates. Then he goes.

The Ododi boy is taller than Dapo and his

muscles are bigger. Grandmummy is a short, old lady. But Dapo knows who he is more afraid of!

"Lockdown is gone!" Mrs Shaky-Shaky changes the subject quickly. "It is finished – pata-pata!"

Everybody claps happily.

Then Mrs Abdul goes to get a tray of fried chicken she has prepared. Grandmummy asks Moji to fetch the moi-moi. And Mrs Raheen tells her boy to start roasting corn.

Now it is a party!

Tola sits on the stairs with her mouth turned down. She is not in a party mood any more. Mrs Shaky-Shaky comes to stand next to Tola on her shaky-shaky legs.

"Don't mind that Ododi boy," she says. "Wait till you tell your friends at school about the Diamonds. You will be a celebrity!"

Tola does not want to be a celebrity. She does not like everybody looking at her. But she does not want to be called a liar either. That is much worse.

Mrs Shaky-Shaky looks past Tola towards the stairs.

"Before lockdown I used to come down from my room every-every day," she says.

Tola nods. At least once a day Mrs Shaky-Shaky came down to talk to whoever was around. She would sit on the outside steps and everybody who passed would stop and talk to her.

"Now it is too hard," Mrs Shaky-Shaky continues. "My legs refuse to cooperate."

Both Tola and Mrs Shaky-Shaky sigh. What problems there are in life!

Then Mrs Shaky-Shaky smiles at Tola.

"Go and eat," she says. "I am going up to my room to rest. You go and enjoy."

So Tola goes and sits with Dapo and three young men who have moved into a room together on the bottom corridor. They are Dapo's new friends.

Tola eats moi-moi and chicken and corn with them. And her party mood comes back.

"What is that old lady doing?" one of Dapo's friends asks.

Tola looks up. He is pointing at Mrs Shaky-Shaky. She is still at the bottom of the stairs. She keeps raising a leg towards the bottom step. But it is too shaky to land there.

"She is trying to go to her room." Tola says.

"So why not just go?" The young man asks.

"Her legs are too shaky," Tola realizes.

The young man smiles.

"What she needs is professional help!" he says.

The young man
goes to Mrs Shaky-
Shaky and picks her up.
Everybody's mouths drop open.
But before anybody can shout
the young man has carried Mrs
Shaky-Shaky to the top of
the stairs.

"My friend's job is carrying sand from the
bottom of the lagoons." Dapo laughs.

"We are professionals at carrying!" One of the
young men announces.

At the top of the stairs Mrs Shaky-Shaky's
head is waggling so fast Tola can hear her false
teeth clacking.

"Thank you, young man," she says at last.

Everybody cheers. Everybody except for
Grandmummy.

"Any fool can carry," she says to the young
man. "Bags of sand are one thing, people are

another. Did you ask if she wanted a lift before you scared the teeth out of her head?"

The young man hung his head.

"Sorry, Ma, sorry," he says.

Grandmummy sucks her teeth and turns away. Dapo looks worried.

On Monday Tola goes back to school. She leaves the room with a smile on her face.

But she comes home with her mouth turned down.

"What is it?" Grandmummy asks.

"Nothing Grandmummy," Tola answers.

"Nothing, abi?"

Grandmummy looks disbelieving – but she hands Tola a plastic container without asking any more.

"Help me take this food to Mrs Shaky-Shaky," she says.

Tola takes the plastic container and walks

down the corridor to Mrs Shaky-Shaky's room.

Mrs Shaky-Shaky greets Tola.

"I cannot go down any more," she says. "As of today my legs are too shaky. Now my friends must come to me…"

She pats Tola's head.

"And here you are!" She smiles.

Tola nods but her mouth refuses to smile.

Mrs Shaky-Shaky offers Tola a biscuit.

Tola chews and swallows as if she is eating a dried-up piece of old stockfish.

Mrs Shaky-Shaky looks worried.

"Something happen for school?" she asks.

Tola opens her mouth to say "Nothing!" – but instead she bursts into tears!

Mrs Shaky-Shaky waits for Tola's tears to slow down before she asks,

"What is wrong my small friend?"

"Nobody believes me," Tola wails. "Nobody at school believes I worked for the Diamonds. Now they are all calling me a liar too!"

Mrs Shaky-Shaky pats Tola's hand gently.

"I believe you!" she says. "And I am sure that your grandmother does. Does she not?"

Tola nods her head, weeping.

"Well, that is two," Mrs Shaky-Shaky says. "Two people who believe you. And I am sure you can count more. If you like counting…"

Tola sniffs back her tears. She definitely likes counting!

Then she hears Grandmummy shouting down the corridor.

"Tola! Tola! Help me fetch water."

"Don't forget to count," Mrs Shaky-Shaky says as Tola runs from the room.

Tola takes the jerry can from Grandmummy. She counts all the way down the stairs to the pump.

Moji, Dapo, Mr Abdul, Mrs Abdul…

Soon Tola reaches ten! Ten people who believe her!

On Tuesday Tola goes back to school with her head held high. But when she comes home she cries again on Mrs Shaky-Shaky's lap.

"Nobody wants to be my friend any more," she sobs. "They say they don't want to be friends with a liar."

Mrs Shaky-Shaky shakes her head sadly.

"A solution must be found," she says. "Everybody needs friends. Even I, who am old, need friends. But now I am stuck up here I cannot get down to them!"

Tola looks at Mrs Shaky-Shaky. Her face looks sad and old and lonely.

A solution must be found for Mrs Shaky-Shaky too, Tola thinks.

Tola is good at finding solutions in maths. But can she find a solution for loneliness? Tola is not sure.

Maths has rules that show how to find the correct solution. Does life have rules too? Tola does not know. She needs to think about it quietly.

But when Tola goes back their room Grandmummy is busy shouting.

"Where is that boy? Where is he?" she shouts.

Tola stops in the doorway. Moji looks up from her borrowed computer.

"Dapo," Moji mouths.

"Where is he?" Grandmummy continues at top volume.

Just then Dapo appears behind Tola.

He takes one look at Grandmummy and freezes.

"Where have you been?" Grandmummy puts her hands on her hips.

Dapo opens his mouth.

"You have been with those boys," Grandmummy answers for him.

"Boys?" Dapo asks innocently.

"You know who I mean!" Grandmummy glares at him. "Those useless, ye-ye, good-for-nothing—"

"Oh those boys!" says Dapo.

They all know Grandmummy means Dapo's new friends. She says they are too old for him.

"They will lead you into trouble," Grandmummy shouts.

Dapo hangs his head.

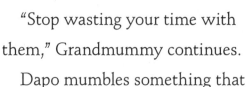

"Stop wasting your time with them," Grandmummy continues.

Dapo mumbles something that sounds like, "Yes, Grandmummy."

"Good," says Grandmummy. "Now let us go to the shopping centre. What are you waiting for?"

Grandmummy sails out of the room with her best handbag on her arm and Dapo trails behind her.

Tola flops down on the bed to think. She is sorry for Dapo. But at least he has friends – unlike her.

On Wednesday after school Tola takes Mrs Shaky-Shaky her food.

"Have you found a solution?" Mrs Shaky-Shaky asks.

Tola hangs her head. She has not yet found a solution for Mrs Shaky-Shaky's loneliness. She has thought both hard and quiet but the rules in life are not so clear as those in maths.

On Thursday Tola sees Mrs Abdul coming up the stairs.

"Are you going to see Mrs Shaky-Shaky?" Mrs Abdul asks.

Tola nods.

"Good girl," Mrs Abdul smiles. "Let us go together."

Baby Jide claps his hands. And Mrs Abdul laughs.

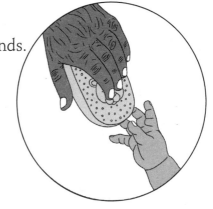

"He loves going to see Mrs Shaky-Shaky," she says. "She always gives him a biscuit!"

Mrs Shaky-Shaky happily gives out biscuits, but she looks so sad when it is time for them go that Tola knows she must find the solution.

On Friday Tola dares to interrupt Moji at her homework. Moji can answer 98% of all questions correctly.

"Life does not have rules like maths does," Moji pronounces.

Tola opens her eyes wide in alarm. If life has no rules does that mean some problems have no solutions? She opens her mouth to ask Moji.

"Shh," Moji says. "Let me study now."

Tola closes her mouth. Grandmummy has said that nobody must interrupt Moji – not unless they want trouble – which Tola does not.

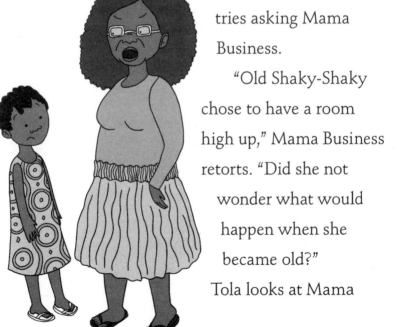

On Saturday Tola even tries asking Mama Business.

"Old Shaky-Shaky chose to have a room high up," Mama Business retorts. "Did she not wonder what would happen when she became old?"

Tola looks at Mama

Business. Does she wonder what will happen when she too gets old? She does not have a downstairs room either!

On Sunday Tola goes to see Mrs Shaky-Shaky with Grandmummy after church. Tola munches a biscuit while the grown-ups talk about their friends.

She is glad that Mrs Shaky-Shaky does not mention Tola's problems at school. She does not want Grandmummy to know about them. Grandmummy would worry. And she would tell Tola that her school friends are good-for-nothings. And that would not make Tola feel better.

Mrs Shaky-Shaky sighs when Grandmummy finishes telling her everything.

"I used to know all the news," she says. "I used to sit on the steps and everybody would talk to me. Now I am just here, looking at these walls."

Grandmummy pats Mrs Shaky-Shaky's hand.

"Old age is not easy," she says.

"It is not easy," Mrs Shaky-Shaky agrees.

On their way back to their room Tola says,

"We must help Mrs Shaky-Shaky!"

"She is my old friend," Grandmummy says sadly. "If I knew how to help I would have already done it."

On Monday after school Tola takes Mrs Shaky-Shaky her food as usual.

"Have you found a solution yet?" Mrs Shaky-Shaky asks hopefully.

Tola shakes her head.

"Sorry, Ma," she says.

"Why are you sorry?" Mrs Shaky-Shaky asks in surprise.

"Because I do not know how to bring you to your friends," Tola says.

"Unless –" Tola puts her head on one side – "unless I ask those big boys to carry you up and down."

Mrs Shaky-Shaky shrieks.

"You want to kill me?" she asks. "You want all my teeth to fall out?"

Tola hangs her head.

Mrs Shaky-Shaky smiles and pats Tola's hand.

"Don't worry about me," she says. "It is you I am worrying about. It is a solution for your problem at school that I want to find."

"Oh!" says Tola quietly. Then she says, "There is no solution."

"Nonsense," Mrs Shaky-Shaky says firmly. "There is always a solution."

But Tola does not believe her. Life does not have rules, Moji has said so. And without rules there are no solutions. Maths has taught Tola that!

When Tola goes home Grandmummy is shouting at Dapo again.

"Why are you late?" she roars. "Who were you with?"

"Nobody," Dapo mutters.

"Nobody, eh?" Grandmummy narrows her eyes. "You are right. Those thick-leg boys are nothing but nobodies."

Tola covers her mouth with her hand so Grandmummy cannot see her laugh.

Grandmummy is right about Dapo's friends legs. They all have big muscles from wading in and out of the lagoon carrying baskets of heavy sand all day long.

They are the ones who should have an upstairs room, Tola thinks. They could run up and down the stairs all day long without tiring.

Then Tola thinks – OH!

"Dapo!" she exclaims.

But Dapo has run from the room.

Tola runs after him. She can guess where he has gone.

"Dapo!" Tola bangs on the door of his friends' room. "Dapo!"

One of the young men answers the door.

"Who says he is here?" he asks.

Tola points past the young man to where Dapo is hiding. The young man laughs.

"She can see you!" he says over his shoulder.

Dapo comes to the door.

"Oh," he says. "It is just you. I thought it was Grandmummy."

"Never mind Grandmummy," Tola says. "Listen!"

Tola tells Dapo her idea. Dapo grins. Then he turns around and explains it to his friends.

"Why not?" they say shrugging and smiling.

Tola claps her hands.

"Thank you! Thank you! Thank you!" she says jumping up and down.

Then Tola, Dapo and the young men run up to Mrs Shaky-Shaky's room. She smiles to see them all.

Tola takes Mrs Shaky-Shaky's hand.

"These boys have a bottom room," she explains. "And they will swap it for your room."

Mrs Shaky-Shaky's eyes open wide. She looks at Tola.

"For true?" she whispers.

Tola nods. Mrs Shaky-Shaky looks at the young men. They grin back at her.

"They don't mind the stairs?" Mrs Shaky-Shaky asks, concerned.

The young men roar with laughter. Tola shakes her head.

"They don't mind at-all at-all," she says.

"O-ya," says one of the young men. "Le's go!"

"Now?" Mrs Shaky-Shaky is alarmed.

"Why not?" he answers.

"But … my things, nko?" Mrs Shaky-Shaky asks nervously. "They are too heavy to move."

The young men look at Mrs Shaky-Shaky's bed and wardrobe and kitchen table. They laugh again. Then they pick up the bed, mattress and all and carry it out of the room.

Mrs Shaky-Shaky cannot believe her eyes.

"Come on!" says Tola.

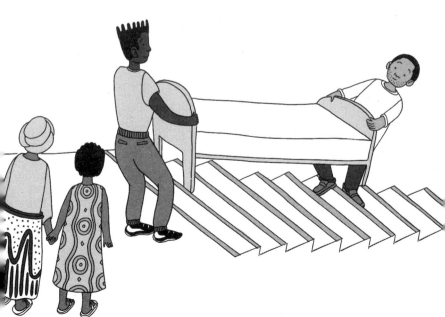

She takes Mrs Shaky-Shaky's hand and gently leads her out of the room.

"The boys will bring everything," Tola says.

Tola and Mrs Shaky-Shaky make their way down the corridor. Mrs Shaky-Shaky keeps her eyes on the floor to make sure her feet land there.

The young men run past on their way back to Mrs Shaky-Shaky's room. They are carrying their bed mats and their wash buckets and their clothes boxes.

"Na-wa-oh!" Mrs Shaky-Shaky says admiringly.

When the young men pass Grandmummy's door it opens.

"Who is running here?" Grandmummy shouts.

"Good evening, Ma," the young men call.

"I should have known it was you!" Grandmummy shouts crossly.

Mrs Shaky-Shaky looks up and notices Grandmummy.

"Have you met these boys?" She smiles. "Such good boys!"

Mrs Shaky-Shaky tells Grandmummy about how the young men are helping her.

Grandmummy begins to look like a frog as she listens. Her eyes bulge and her mouth stretches out to her ears.

Tola tries not to laugh.

"Come on, Tola," Mrs Shaky-Shaky concludes. "Let me see my new room!"

Tola and Mrs Shaky-Shaky slowly walk on.

It takes a long time to get to the bottom room. Mrs Shaky-Shaky needs help on the stairs. And she stops to tell everybody what is happening.

Mrs Abdul claps her hands for joy.

But Mama Business says, "Those boys will break your things carrying them. And what they do not break they will steal."

Mrs Shaky-Shaky looks at Tola nervously.

But when they get to the bottom room Mrs Shaky-Shaky's things are all there in one piece. And placed just like they were in her old room.

"Thank you, boys!" Mrs Shaky-Shaky cries. "God bless you!"

"Don't worry, Ma, don't worry!"

The boys bow politely and run off to where Dapo is waiting in their new room.

Mrs Shaky-Shaky turns to Tola.

"Tola! You are a good friend!" She wipes her eyes. "You found a solution for me!"

Tola smiles with her whole face.

Mrs Shaky-Shaky leans over and grips Tola's shoulder.

"There will be a solution for you too," she says.

Tola hangs her head. She found a solution for Mrs Shaky-Shaky by chance. But without rules to follow how can she find a solution for herself?

"Tola! Tola!" Grandmummy is shouting from upstairs.

"O-ya, go on," Mrs Shaky-Shaky smiles.

Tola hugs her friend then runs up the stairs to her room.

And there – sitting on the floor – are the three young men!

Tola cannot believe her eyes!

Grandmummy looks up from the gas. She is stirring her famous okra soup.

"O-ya, Tola," she says. "Help me borrow bowls from Mrs Abdul. These boys need to eat. They have worked hard."

Now Tola cannot believe her ears!

"Did you not hear me?" Grandmummy asks. "Why are you just standing there?"

Tola runs out of the room. She passes Dapo in the corridor.

"Have you seen my friends?" he asks.

"They are with Grandmummy," Tola says.

Now Dapo looks afraid.

"What is she doing to them?" he asks with wide eyes.

Tola giggles.

"Go and see," she says, pushing Dapo towards their room.

Then Tola realizes – she not only found a solution for Mrs Shaky-Shaky's problem – she found one for Dapo too!

And maybe, maybe, maybe ... that means that there is a solution to her problem too!

Tola Counts the Uncountable

Tola lives in a room in a run-down block of flats in the megacity of Lagos.

In Lagos there are millionaires who own houses on paradise islands, where they go for holidays.

And in Lagos there are people who are happy if they get a day off now and then.

One day Grandmummy announces, "We are going to take a holiday!"

Moji and Dapo and Tola all stare at Grandmummy. They have never taken a holiday before.

"Like to Monaco?" Moji asks slowly, fanning herself with an exercise book.

Moji has a scholarship to a fancy school on the island. Girls at her school go on holiday to millionaire places like Monaco.

Dapo roars with laughter. And Grandmummy sucks her teeth.

"Has that school erased your common sense?" she asks scornfully.

Grandmummy might never have been to school but she knows exactly how far her money can reach. And it will not reach Monaco!

"A holiday … like a church vigil?" Dapo asks.

Ladies often go to their church to pray with other church ladies. Some ladies pray for days. Crying children and complaining husbands cannot disturb them when they are on a church vigil.

Grandmummy frowns at Dapo.

"Kneeling on a church floor for three days and three nights is not a holiday!" she snaps.

"Do you mean –" Tola suggests the only thing she can think of – "the beach?"

A look of relief crosses Grandmummy's sweating face.

"That is exactly what I was going to say," she says. "We are going to the beach!"

Grandmummy beams at their hot, sweaty faces. It is over 40 degrees outside, and inside their one room it is far, far hotter.

"It is breezy at the beach," she says. "We will be cool!"

Moji shrugs.

"We could cool down right here if we had an air conditioner," she says.

Grandmummy raises her eyebrows. She looks like she is going to say something else about Moji's common sense. But Moji speaks first.

"The beach is good," she says quickly. "There are umbrellas and loungers, and waiters to bring you food and drink."

Tola's mouth perks up at the corners.

"But it costs five thousand naira to enter," Moji frowns.

Tola's mouth turns down again.

"Our beach is free!" Grandmummy says firmly. "And we are going. On Saturday."

Tola's mouth perks up again.

"Saturday? This Saturday?" Moji says. "I cannot go this Saturday. I have a meeting with my mentor."

"And I have a football match," says Dapo.

Tola sighs. Grandmummy will not let Moji

42

miss a meeting with her mentor. And she will not force Dapo to miss a football match either, not when he works so hard all week.

Tola's mouth turns down – it joins her heart, downcast because of her problems at school.

Grandmummy notices. She lifts Tola's chin.

"We will still go," she says. "Just you and me."

"For true?" Tola looks up at Grandmummy.

Grandmummy looks at Tola's hopeful mouth. She nods determinedly.

"Saturday," she says. "We are going to the beach!"

Tola's mouth turns all the way up taking her

heart with it. Once Grandmummy has made up her mind only a government decree can change it.

Tola wants to tell everybody at school that she is going to the beach. But she knows they will just call her a liar again.

So Tola stands silently in the blazing hot playground. She watches all the other children play with each other. And she imagines lying under an umbrella in the breeze. She imagines the waiters who will listen to her politely and bring her whatever she asks for and not call her names.

On Saturday, Tola is ready before Grandmummy even gets out of bed. She is wearing her best dress and her plastic necklace. Grandmummy smiles.

"Take some food to Mrs Shaky-Shaky," she says. "I will collect you from there."

So Tola runs down to Mrs Shaky-Shaky's new bottom room. She tells her all about the umbrellas and the loungers and the waiters.

Mrs Shaky-Shaky is very impressed.

"Beaches were not like that in my day," she says. "There was just sand and coconut trees and waves."

Waves! Tola's eyes open wide in alarm.

Tola had imagined the comfortable loungers. She had imagined the colourful umbrellas. She had even imagined the smart waiters. But she had not thought even once about waves!

Would they be big? Would they be dangerous? Would they catch her?

Before Tola can ask about the waves Grandmummy arrives and hurries her along. They hurry out of the flats, across the rough ground, and along the busy road.

Grandmummy does not want to miss even one minute of their holiday. And neither does Tola! They smile as they hurry along. And they even smile as they squeeze onto a crowded danfo minibus.

The danfo is packed with hot sweaty people.

There are loud women going to market with shopping baskets on their heads. There are quiet office workers in smart suits with their noses in the air. There are children running errands for their parents – delivering boxes and bags and animals to relatives on the other side of the city.

Grandmummy and Tola smile again at each other. They are not on their way to work or

chores – they are on their way to the beach!

The bus crawls along in the traffic. Grandmummy and Tola sweat more and more and more. Grandmummy has to take Tola onto her lap so that Tola does not have to stand nose to nose with a goat!

When the bus reaches the market some women get off. But many more get on with huge bags and baskets of shopping.

At last the bus reaches Carter Bridge. By now some of the children have got off one by one by one with their chickens and their goats. But not the one that's eyeing Tola!

Grandmummy sighs. There is no room for her to stretch out her legs. Tola looks at Grandmummy's feet. The heat has made them swell out of her best shoes.

When the bus crosses the big bridge onto the island some of the office workers get off – but others get on.

Grandmummy sighs again. She tries to take her fan out of her handbag and fan her sweating face without poking anyone with her fan or her elbow.

On the island there are big holes in the road. Holes big enough to swallow a hippopotamus.

The bus driver drives slowly, but still the bus leans from side to side as if it will fall over at any minute.

"Can dey not repair de road?" One of the women exclaims loudly.

"Where is the money for roads?" A man asks annoyed.

"De money dey but de minister for transport

chop-am!" a young man responds.

"'E done buy himself one paradise island," a young woman confirms.

She holds up her phone with a picture of an island that the minister has posted.

The people on the bus mutter angrily. They clutch the seats in front of them so they don't fall onto the floor as the bus dives into another hole.

"This our country-o!" Grandmummy shakes her head.

Grandmummy is not smiling any more. But Tola is.

She does not mind that the bus is as hot as a soldier ant's bite. She does not mind that the bus is as slow as a tortoise. She does not mind that the bus is as bumpy as a camel. Because this bus is taking her to the beach!

Finally Grandmummy stands up. It is their turn to get off the bus.

As soon as she climbs down Tola looks excitedly left and right – but all she can see are huge blocks of flats surrounded by flowering gardens. Tola clutches Grandmummy's arm. Are they lost?

Grandmummy puts her hand out into the road. An okada taxi driver makes an emergency stop.

"Take us to the beach!" Grandmummy orders.

Tola gasps.

Grandmummy has forbidden Moji and Dapo and Tola to ride okadas. She says motorbikes are dangerous and okada drivers are reckless and rude.

Grandmummy looks at Tola with one eyebrow raised.

"There is one rule for every day," she says firmly. "And another rule for holidays."

Tola frowns. Rules do not change. At least not in maths.

But Tola does not argue. She has always wanted to ride an okada!

The okada driver passes Grandmummy and Tola a helmet each.

"You better carry me and my granddaughter safely or I will kill you myself," Grandmummy says to him.

"Yes, Ma!" he replies as meekly as a fly in the mouth of a lizard.

Tola grins.

A breeze blows in Tola's face as the motor-bike zooms off down the road. She beams. This breeze is one million times better than goat's breath!

Too soon the okada driver stops.

"We have arrived," he says.

Tola looks around eagerly for the umbrellas and loungers and waiters.

But all she can see is a low wall where many hawkers are sitting. They are selling oranges and groundnuts and roasted corn.

On the other side of the wall is some flat ground covered in rubbish.

"We are here!" Grandmummy announces. "The beach!"

"But—" Tola's face creases like an overripe tomato.

"What?" Grandmummy waits for Tola to speak.

Then Tola sees how Grandmummy's smile

is proud and bright even though her feet have swollen, her blouse is wet with sweat, and her face is tired. She is holding her smile out to Tola like a balloon.

"Nothing, Grandmummy," Tola says quickly.

And Tola forces her mouth to turn up at the corners. Grandmummy has suffered to get them here. And Tola is not going to burst Grandmummy's smile.

But Tola cannot force her heart up. Nobody can do that.

Tola follows Grandmummy along the wall. She looks at the beach covered with rubbish. Now she knows why this beach is free.

Moji goes to school with girls who have money to pay for beaches with loungers and umbrellas and waiters. They are so lucky!

Grandmummy stops next to a hawker who is

frying akara. She takes a handkerchief out of her handbag and spreads it on the wall. Then she sits down on it with a thankful sigh.

"Now go and play," she says to Tola. "Go and play on the beach."

Grandmummy points to the rubbish. Underneath the rubbish is sand.

"Just don't go near the sea." Grandmummy warns.

Tola lifts her eyes up and sees for the first time a blue that touches the sky. A blue that stretches to both corners of the world. A blue that booms!

Tola takes a step closer to Grandmummy.

"She is afraid," the hawker laughs.

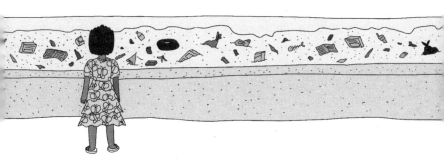

Grandmummy turns to the hawker and frowns.

"Nonsense," she says. "She is hungry. You better cook for us quick-quick."

"Yes, Ma!" the hawker says.

She turns back to her frying pan and plops some akara batter into the hot oil.

Grandmummy chuckles happily.

Grandmummy used to squat in the hot sun roasting groundnuts for impatient customers. Those days are gone now Dapo is working. And Tola knows that Grandmummy thanks God for that.

The smell of frying akara enters Tola's nose and she sniffs eagerly. Grandmummy was right. She is hungry!

Soon Tola and Grandmummy are munching happily. Then Grandmummy

calls over a boy with a basket of coconuts on his head.

"Cut two for us," she says to him. "We are thirsty."

"Yes, Ma!" says the boy.

He cuts the top off a coconut, puts a straw inside it and hands it to Tola.

She takes it eagerly. Grandmummy was right again. Tola is thirsty!

"Now go and play on the beach," Grandmummy says firmly.

Tola looks at the things the waves have thrown up onto the sand.

There are plastic bottles, broken barrels, torn nets, plastic bags, old ropes, odd flip-flops, spoilt toys, and many unrecognizable things.

Worst of all are the waves in the distance. What if one of them were to catch Tola

up and throw her down onto a beach on the
other side of the world?

Tola does not want to take one step away
from Grandmummy.

But the hawker laughs again. So Tola puts one
foot out onto the rubbish. And then another.

"Just do not go into the water. You hear me?"
Grandmummy says.

Tola nods. She does not even want to look at
those waves.

Tola stirs the rubbish with her toe.
Underneath there is sand. It glitters and
glimmers in the hot sun.

Tola stirs the dirt with her finger. Underneath
the grains of sand is more and more and more
sand.

How many grains of sand are on this
beach? Tola wonders.

More than there are cars. More than there are people. More than there are cockroaches in the whole entire city of Lagos.

Tola could count the cars. She could count the people. She could even count the cockroaches – if she could get them to stop scuttling about and stand still. But Tola knows she could never ever count all the sand on this one beach!

There are enough numbers – but there would never be enough time! Numbers are infinite – they go on forever. Tola knows this – but she had not known that there existed things too lengthy to count.

Just then a group of shouting children run past Tola. She looks up. Five shouting children run right across the rubbish and straight into the waves.

Tola's mouth drops open.

As she watches the children run up to their knees in the waves and then run out again.

They do it again and again shouting happily.
And the waves do not carry the children away
– not even one of them. Tola knows, because
there are still five of them.

Tola stares at the children for a long time.

The sand is burning her feet through her
flip-flops. Sweat is itching her face and her back.
And the sun is cooking her head.

Tola looks over her shoulder.

Grandmummy has put a
newspaper over her
face. She has put her
feet up on an old broken
bucket. Grandmummy
is sleeping.

So Tola takes one step. Then she takes another … and another … and another … until she has crossed the rubbish and the sea is right in front of her.

Far out, the big blue waves are booming. But closer, little white whispering waves are running up the sand.

Tola looks over her shoulder again. Grandmummy is still sleeping.

She looks back at the laughing splashing children. The waves are still not carrying them away.

So Tola takes one step forward. And a tiny wave covers her toes. The water is so cool and so fresh that Tola's toes wriggle as if they are dancing.

Tola's toes are so happy that they dance Tola forwards until the waves are lapping at Tola's hot ankles.

Tola's feet feel so good that Tola laughs out loud. Then something grabs Tola's ear –

"Aie!" Tola shrieks.

She looks up. Grandmummy is holding Tola's ear and glaring down at her.

"I told you to stay away from—" Grandmummy shouts.

Then Grandmummy's mouth drops open. Her eyes bulge. And slowly Grandmummy looks down at her feet. Her swollen ankles are being tickled by cool water.

Tola waits for Grandmummy to drag her by the ear away from the sea.

But Grandmummy is watching her toes wriggle.

She lets go of Tola's ear, bends down and takes off her shoes.

"Ahhhh…" says Grandmummy. A look of joy crosses her face. Grandmummy closes her eyes.

When she opens them again she holds out her hand to Tola.

"Let us walk in the water," she says.

Tola looks up at Grandmummy in confusion.

"Holiday rules." Grandmummy smiles.

Tola still does not approve of rules changing. But she likes the holiday rules better than the every day rules. So once again she does not complain.

Grandmummy and Tola walk along the beach in the cool whispering waves. They walk until the waves have washed away all their worries. They walk until they are cool.

And the waves never stop coming.

Waves, Tola realizes, are as uncountable as the tiny grains of sand.

But the waves are cool. And the sand is firm. And Grandmummy is holding Tola's hand. Because she loves her.

Grandmummy's love is uncountable too, Tola

thinks. Infinite numbers show that infinite things do exist. Infinite and uncountable things – like love.

Too Small Tola Is a Rock Star

Too Small Tola lives in Lagos, unbelievable Lagos.

In Lagos there are children who live in mansions. Mansions so big their parents have to call their children's mobile phones to find which room they are in!

And in Lagos there are children who sleep on cardboard boxes under bridges where people step over them both day and night.

Tola's family are lucky. They do not own a mansion or even a flat. But they do not sleep under bridges either. They are lucky enough to have the roof of one room over their heads.

Sometimes though they do not feel so lucky!

"Dapo!" Moji hisses. "Stop snoring!"

"Shh!" says Grandmummy.

"I am trying to sleep!" Moji complains. "I have a test to study for."

"So get up and study and let the rest of us sleep," Dapo mutters.

"But it is still night!" Moji whines.

Tola puts her fingers in her ears.

"It is no longer night!" Grandmummy snaps. "Can you not hear the cocks crowing?"

Moji groans.

"Just get up!" Grandmummy orders.

Moji gets up – and trips over Dapo. He is on his mat on the floor.

"Aiieeee!" Dapo shouts. "You want to kill me?"

"Now what?" Grandmummy sucks her teeth.

"She kicked me!" Dapo complains. "And I was sleeping!"

Tola puts a pillow over her face.

"It is morning," Moji says brightly. "Why are you sleeping if it is morning?"

"Jus' shut up!" Dapo shouts.

Just then there is a gentle knock on the door.

Tola remembers she is supposed to be looking after baby Jide today while Mrs Abdul goes to help Mr Abdul with his customers!

She jumps up and opens the door a crack.

"*Salam Alekum,*" says Mrs Abdul.

"Peace be with you too, Mrs Abdul," Tola smiles back.

"Are you ready to come?" Mrs Abdul asks.

"Yes," Tola says. "I will come now-now."

Tola shuts the door. She changes out of her night wrapper, and brushes her teeth at top speed.

"Breakfast, nko?" Grandmummy asks as Tola runs out of the door.

"No time!" Tola shouts.

She runs down the corridor and down the stairs to the Abduls' room.

"Tola!" Mr Abdul says. "Welcome!"

Baby Jide sees Tola.
He shuffles on his bom-bom
towards her with his
nappy rubbing along the floor.

"Look at him crawl!"
Mr Abdul says proudly.
"This boy could win
Olympic medals for his crawling!"

Mrs Abdul laughs.

"He is just happy to see Tola," she says.

Tola smiles. She is happy to see him too. Tola
loves baby Jide. He is small and fat, with hands
like stars and a smile as sweet as a mango.

Baby Jide reaches his hands up to Tola. And
suddenly tears jump into Tola's eyes.

At school her friends won't hold her hand any
more. They say, who wants to hold hands with
a liar?

Tola has to look up at the sky to hold back her
tears when they say that.

But baby Jide continues to hold out his hands and smile. So Tola blinks away her tears and picks him up. Baby Jide's smile grows wider than ever.

But when Mr and Mrs Abdul leave, baby Jide's mouth starts to wobble.

Quickly Tola builds a tower on the floor with some metal bowls. Baby Jide loves towers. He loves to makes them come crashing down!

CRASH!

"'Gen! 'gen!" baby Jide shouts.

Tola builds the tower again and again and again. Each time baby Jide pushes it over with a big CRASH. Then he shouts with happiness and claps his hands.

Suddenly the door bursts open. Tola leaps up.

"What is all this noise?"
Mama Business demands.

She stands in the open
doorway with her hands
on her hips.

"Sorry, Ma," says Tola.
"We are only playing."

"That is no excuse!"
Mama Business snaps.

Tola hangs her head.

"I did not want him to cry," she says.

"Let him cry," Mama Business orders. "That is
how he will learn to be good."

Tola knows it is rude to argue. So she stays
good and quiet.

Mama Business tells Tola how to look after
babies – yaka-yaka, yaka-yaka, yaka-yaka.

"… that is how I raised my babies," Mama
Business concludes. "I let them cry and I took no
notice."

"Yes, Ma," Tola says.

She has often wondered why none of Mama Business's children or grandchildren come to visit. And now she knows.

"So don't let me hear that noise again!" Mama Business orders.

"Yes, Ma," Tola says again.

Mama Business leaves at last. Tola shuts the door and sighs. She turns around saying to baby Jide, "Let's play sleeping lions instead."

But where is baby Jide?

Tola can see the whole room – the bed, the kitchen bowls and buckets, the boxes of clothes in the corner.

But no baby Jide! Is he playing hide and seek?

"Jide!" Tola calls looking under the bed.

But baby Jide is not there. Where could he have gone? There is nowhere else to hide!

And there is nowhere for him to go … unless … unless he crawled out of the room while

Mama Business was standing in the open doorway!

"Baby Jide!" Tola shouts in fear.

She runs out into the corridor. She looks up and she looks down but she cannot see a baby anywhere.

All she can see are doors. Some doors are closed. Some doors are open. Has baby Jide gone into one of the neighbours' rooms?

"Jide!" Tola calls again.

Baby Jide does not answer.

There is only the faint sound of Mrs Shaky-Shaky's radio from her room downstairs.

Tola runs down the corridor. When she comes to an open door she looks inside.

There is deaf old Mr Commot snoozing in his chair. There is an  old broken television on a table. And there are some buckets in the corner. The buckets are lying on their sides. As if they have just been knocked over…

Tola shouts, "Jide!"

Mr Commot does not wake. And Tola can see Jide is no longer there.

She runs down the corridor to the next open door. Her heart is beating faster than a talking drum!

She looks inside the room. Mrs Raheen is in there. She is pouring water into small plastic bags. Her children are waiting to go and sell the water bags to thirsty people on the hot streets.

Tola looks among them. But she cannot see baby Jide.

"Baby Jide?" Tola asks.

"Eh?" Mrs Raheen asks back.

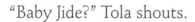

She cannot hear Tola because Mrs Shaky-Shaky has turned the song on her radio up so loud.

"Baby Jide?" Tola shouts.

Mrs Raheen and her children shake their heads. They have not seen baby Jide.

Tola runs down the corridor. She can hear shouting and fighting coming from the next open door. It is the Ododis' room. The Ododi boys love to fight. And if they cannot fight anyone else, then they fight each other.

Tola peeps around the door. Legs are kicking, arms are punching, voices are shouting. But none of those arms and legs belong to a small, fat baby.

Tola crouches down to pass the open door. She does not want the Ododi boys to see her! But on the dirty corridor floor she sees a thick smudgy line.

It is not the thin line of Mr Abdul's bicycle wheels. It is not the smudgy footprints of the neighbours. And it is not the round marks of footballs that are supposedly banned in the corridors.

Tola stares hard at that long thick smudgy line.

It looks just like the sort of mark a baby might make if he was wriggling along on his bom-bom with his nappy rubbing along the corridor floor.

Tola looks back. The line comes from Mr Commot's room. And from Mr Commot's room the line goes straight back to the Abduls' door.

Baby Jide must have made the mark! And it heads straight for the stairs!

"Aieee!" Tola shouts.

What if baby Jide has fallen down the stairs?

Tola shouts so loudly the Ododi boys stop fighting. But she runs so fast that when they look around there is no one there. Tola is already running down the stairs.

There are a lot of neighbours crowded around the bottom of the stairs!

"Aieee!" Tola shouts again.

What if they are looking at baby Jide?

But the neighbours do not look worried. They look happy. They are singing and dancing to the song on Mrs Shaky-Shaky's radio.

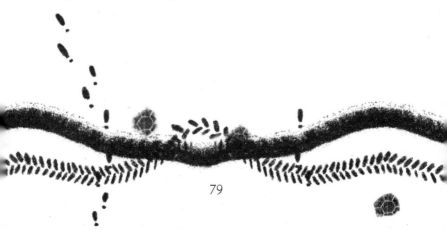

"Baby Jide?" Tola shouts to them over the music.

The neighbours clap and cheer when they see Tola.

"Baby Jide?" Tola shouts again.

The neighbours smile and shrug.

Tola's heart beats fast.

What if baby Jide has crawled past them and out onto the street?

"Tola!" Mrs Shaky-Shaky shouts.

Tola turns around and through her open door Tola sees—

Baby Jide!

He is sitting on the floor eating a biscuit in Mrs Shaky-Shaky's room!

"JIDE!" Tola shouts.

She runs into the room, picks up baby Jide, and bursts into tears.

"Tola!" Mrs Shaky-Shaky exclaims. "I thought you would be happy."

"I am happy! I am so so happy!" Tola weeps.

"Everybody is going to believe you now," Mrs Shaky-Shaky shouts over her radio.

Tola does not know what Mrs Shaky-Shaky means. And she does not care.

"I thought I had lost him," she cries.

"Who?" Mrs Shaky-Shaky looks confused.

"Baby Jide," Tola sobs. "I was looking after him. And I lost him."

Mrs Shaky-Shaky looks surprised.

"Baby Jide always comes for a morning biscuit," she says. "Mrs Abdul brings him…"

Mrs Shaky-Shaky looks towards the neighbours dancing in the corridor.

"I thought Mrs Abdul was out there with the others," she says.

Tola shakes her head.

"She went out," she says. "And he crawled here by himself."

"Na-wa-oh!" Mrs Shaky-Shaky laughs.

Tola cannot laugh. She squeezes baby Jide tight. He wriggles and she puts him down.

And then she frowns. Out in the corridor the neighbours are singing along with the song. And it is her name they are singing!

"Tola! Tola!"

Tola opens her eyes wide in surprise.

"What is this song?" she asks.

"This song?" Mrs Shaky-Shaky says beaming. "This song which I recorded from the radio?"

Tola nods.

"Ah!" Mrs Shaky-Shaky announces proudly. "This is the new Diamond song."

She turns the song up even louder. The neighbours cheer.

"One house girl –
Tola! Tola!
A very clever one –
Tola! Tola!
Counting up –
Tola! Tola!
Up to Mars –
Tola! Tola!
Nobody can count like her – ah-ah –
Tola! Tola!"

Tola's eyes open so wide that baby Jide laughs.

"Now everyone will know you were telling the truth," Mrs Shaky-Shaky says happily.

Tola sits down on the floor with a bump. Mrs Shaky-Shaky pats her head with a shaky-shaky hand.

"This is your solution," she says.

Tola listens to the song over and over again. It is playing on every radio station!

When Mr and Mrs Abdul come home from work Tola is still sitting on Mrs Shaky-Shaky's floor. And she is holding baby Jide tightly in her arms. She is feeding him biscuits to stop him wriggling away.

Mr and Mrs Abdul laugh to see them.

"Thank you for looking after our baby!" they say.

Tola hangs her head. They are thanking her for something she did not do! And now they will be angry with her.

"I did not look after him," she says. "I lost him!"

Mr and Mrs Abdul's eyes open wide with fear.

"Mama Business distracted her," Mrs Shaky-Shaky says. "She distracted her from watching baby Jide."

Tola tells them what happened.

"That Mama!" Mrs Abdul exclaims. "She can never mind her own business!"

Then she looks at Tola.

"Baby Jide knows how to come down here," she says. "Usually I just open the door and follow him down."

"I told you." Mr Abdul smiles proudly. "His crawling is Olympic!"

"I should have told you, Tola," Mrs Abdul says. "Then you would have known where to look."

Tola is so relieved that they are not angry with her that she starts to cry.

"Don't worry, Tola." Mr and Mrs Abdul say. "Don't worry. It is not your fault."

They say it again and again until Tola stops crying.

Then they take baby Jide back to their own room.

"Go now," Mrs Shaky-Shaky says to Tola. "Go and tell your grandmother about the song."

Tola throws her arms around Mrs Shaky-Shaky.

"You are my best friend!" she says.

"And you are mine," says Mrs Shaky-Shaky with a shaky-shaky voice.

Then Tola runs out of the room.

"Grandmummy!" she shouts. "Grandmummy!"

Grandmummy, Dapo and Moji are all in their room. They all turn to look at Tola when she runs in. Her song is coming through the open window.

"You hear this?" Dapo shouts as if he cannot believe his ears.

"Did you know?" Moji breathes.

"Tola, Tola…" Grandmummy shakes her head and beams.

Suddenly Tola feels shy.

"Your song! Your own Diamond song!"

Dapo grabs Tola's hands.

"Now that Ododi boy will believe you!" he crows.

Tola beams too.

"Now everybody will believe me," she says shyly.

"Who else did not believe you?" Moji frowns.

"At school." Tola shrugs, as if it was nothing.

"They did not believe you before?" Now Dapo is frowning too.

Tola does not answer. But Grandmummy can guess.

"Have they been tormenting you at school?" she asks slowly.

Tola does not want to answer.

"Now everybody will believe me!" she says happily.

"Who cares about everybody?" Grandmummy frowns.

Tola hangs her head. She cares.

"Those useless ye-ye tormentors…" Grandmummy starts to get angry.

"Now they will be my friends again," Tola interrupts hopefully.

"They are not true friends," Grandmummy says sucking her teeth.

Tola looks at Grandmummy. Maybe she is right…

But Tola is tired of seeing everybody holding hands with everybody else – and nobody holding hands with her. She wants somebody to hold hands with. Even if they are not a true friend.

Suddenly Moji gets up from her computer. She comes and puts her arm around Tola.

Tola looks at Moji in surprise. Moji never gets up from her work. Not unless Grandmummy orders her to do something.

"Your true friends always believed you," Moji says. "And you know who they are now."

Tola nods slowly.

"And you know who is not-so-true," Moji continues.

Tola nods again.

"And it is OK to be friends with all of them," Moji says.

Tola's heart gives a little happy hop.

"Just remember who is who," Moji continues, "and only trust the true ones."

"What use are the others?" Grandmummy asks scornfully.

For fun, Tola thinks. For playing and laughing. But not for trusting, not for counting on.

"They may truly like you," Moji says to Tola, "but not be strong enough to stand up for you."

Grandmummy looks hard at Moji.

"Where did you learn this?" she asks.

"At school," Moji shrugs. "Where else?"

Grandmummy puts her hand on Moji's head. And Dapo pats her arm.

"They mock me for my rough accent and rough clothes and rough  hair," Moji says stiffly, "But when I am a doctor I will make them pay double since they are so rich and fine!

Dapo laughs but Tola does not. She puts her arms around Moji and squeezes her tight.

The sound of Tola's song floats louder through the window. It seems like the whole city is playing it.

"You will be a celebrity at school tomorrow," Dapo says proudly.

"Everybody will want to be your friend." Moji smiles.

"They will all be saying sorry-o sorry-o!" Dapo says.

"And what will you say to those not-so-true friends?" Grandmummy asks.

Tola thinks. She likes the thought of people saying sorry. Maybe sorry is what will make the pain go away?

"Anyone who says sorry can hold my hand," she says.

Grandmummy purses her lips. Dapo pats her back. Moji looks at Tola.

"And when they want your help with maths?" she asks.

Tola thinks for a moment.

"From now on they can all pay me in sweets!"
Tola decides.

Moji laughs. Dapo laughs. Even Grandmummy
laughs. And Tola joins in too. Her worries are over!

"Tola! Tola!" Dapo sings triumphantly.

That night the whole of Lagos is playing Tola's
song.

One house girl – Tola! Tola! A very clever one – Tola! Tola! Counting up – Tola! Tola!

It plays in air-conditioned houses with sound systems, and under the bridges where children sleep.

It plays in the rooms where Tola's classmates live. They listen with hands over their open mouths. They are wishing they could go back and do different. But they cannot. Nobody can. We can only go on.

Go on, make amends, and do different next time.

Tomorrow Tola will accept all the sorry-ohs.

She knows how easy it is to make a mistake. And how important it is to forgive – even if you cannot trust that person again.

Tola does not know if the Abduls will ask her to look after baby Jide again. But what matters most is that they have forgiven her for making a mistake.

The solutions for life's problems are not so easy to find as the solutions in maths. There are no rules to show the way.

But there is thank you, and there is sorry, and there is forgiveness.

And most of all there is love.

Atinuke was born in Nigeria and spent her childhood in both Africa and the UK. She is the author of the bestselling Anna Hibiscus and No. 1 Car Spotter series, as well as *Africa, Amazing Africa: Country by Country*. She started her career as an oral storyteller of tales from the African continent; now she writes about contemporary life in Nigeria. Atinuke lives on a mountain overlooking the sea in West Wales. Visit her website at **atinuke.co.uk**

✺

Onyinye Iwu is Nigerian. She was born in Italy, where she spent most of her childhood, then moved to the UK when she was a teenager.

A teacher by day and an illustrator by night, Onyinye enjoys reading books, especially ones that make her laugh. Visit her website at **onyinyeiwu.com**